A Bilingual Book
English/Español

Scrapbook Stories

Rose Tooley Gamblin
and Oscar Hernandéz

D1475765

Autumn House® Publishing
www.autumnhousepublishing.com
A Division of REVIEW AND HERALD® PUBLISHING
Since 1861

Published by Autumn House® Publishing, a division of Review and Herald®
Publishing, Hagerstown, MD 21741-1119

Autumn House® titles may be purchased in bulk for educational, business, fund-
raising, or sales promotional use. For information, please e-mail
SpecialMarkets@reviewandherald.com.

Autumn House® Publishing publishes biblically based materials for spiritual,
physical, and mental growth and Christian discipleship.

The author assumes full responsibility for the accuracy of all facts and quotations as
cited in this book.

This book was
Edited by Jeannette R. Johnson
Designed by Ron J. Pride
Illustrated by Mary Bausman, Owl Mountain Graphics
Typeset: Clearface Regular 16/18. (Spanish) NB Helvetica Narrow Bold 13/15

PRINTED IN U.S.A.

12 11 10 09 08   5 4 3 2 1

Library of Congress Cataloging-in-Publication Data

Gamblin, Rose Tooley, 1956-
  Bill's lunch = El almuerzo de Bill / Rose Tooley Gamblin ; translated
into Spanish by Oscar Hernandez.
      p. cm.
  Text in English and Spanish.
  "Scrapbook Stories Books."
  Summary: The children decide to play a practical joke on their
classmate Bill, and replace his cold potato with a rock for his lunch,
but Lee, not agreeing with them, switches out the rock for his own lunch.
  ISBN 978-0-8127-0472-3
  [1. Practical jokes--Juvenile Literature. 2. Lunchboxes--Juvenile Literature. 3.
Schools--Juvenile Literature. 4. Spanish language materials--Bilingual.] I.
Hernández, Oscar. II. Title. III. Title: Almuerzo de Bill.
PZ73.G14713 2010

                        2007039016

This book is dedicated to Patrick,
a young boy who is not afraid to stand up for what is right.

I have read this book all by myself!
¡He leído todo este libro!

_____

My Name / Mi Nombre

_____

Date / Fecha

What I Think About This Story
Qué pienso de esta historia

_____

_____

_____

_____

Other *Scrapbook Stories* Books:

The Birthday Party
Jon's Canary

To order, call 1-800-765-6955.

Visit us at www.AutumnHousePublishing.com for
information on other Autumn House® products.

Dear Caring Adult,

This story is adapted from the Scrapbook stories collected by Ellen G. White. In the early years of her work, while absent from her home on long trips, she took time to gather up the best stories she could find for boys and girls. She would often find relaxation in reading and clipping these stories and pasting them in scrapbooks.

This is one of those stories and is based on the story titled, "Joe Green's Lunch." We have selected this story as the second one in a series of stories from Ellen G. White's scrapbooks. It is a story that never grows old, and we know you will find it helpful when you are teaching about friendships.

This series of I-can-read books is designed to be read by the child (with a little help from you). This makes it an ideal book for the emergent reader.

—The Publishers

It was time to play.
"Look at Bill!" said the boys.
"He does not come to play."

Era hora de jugar.
"Miren a Bill," dijeron los muchachos.
"Él no viene a jugar."

"See Bill?" said the girls.
"Bill does not see us.
"We will look in Bill's lunch."

"Vean a Bill," dijeron las muchachas.
"Bill no nos ve"
"Nosotros inspeccionaremos el almuerzo de Bill."

"This is not lunch!" said a boy.
"This is not lunch!" said a girl.
"This is funny!" said a boy.
"This is *not* funny!" said Lee.

"Este no es un almuerzo," dijo un muchacho.
"Este no es un almuerzo," dijo una muchacha.
"Esto es divertido," dijo un muchacho.
"Esto no es divertido," dijo un Lee.

10

"We will have fun," said the boy.
"We will play with Bill's lunch,"
said the boys and girls.
"This is *not* fun!" said Lee.

"Nos divertiremos," dijo el muchacho.
"Jugaremos con el almuerzo de Bill,"
dijeron los muchachos y las muchachas.
"¡Esto no es divertido! Dijo Lee.

"Es hora de leer," dijo la maestra.
Aquí están las muchachas.
Aquí están los muchachos.
¿Pero dónde está Lee?"

"It is time to read," said the teacher.
"Here are the girls.
Here are the boys.
But where is Lee?"

Here is Lee.
He will not play with Bill's lunch.
See what Lee will do.

Aquí está Lee.
Él no jugará con el almuerzo de Bill.
Veamos qué hará Lee.

"It is time to read," said the teacher.
"And here is Lee.
"Lee, will you read?"

"Es hora de leer," dijo la maestra
Y aquí está Lee.
¿Leerá Lee?

It is time for lunch.
See the boys and girls?
They can go.
See the boys and girls go.

Es hora de almuerzo.
¿Ven a los muchachos y las muchachas?
Ellos pueden ir.
Vean a los muchachos y a las muchachas partir.

Bill will get his lunch.
Bill does not know.
Bill will go.

Bill obtendrá su almuerzo.
Bill no sabe.
Bill irá a comer.

"We will see Bill," said the boys and girls.
"We will see Bill at lunch time."

"Veremos a Bill," dijeron los muchachos y las muchachas.
"Veremos a Bill a la hora de almuerzo."

Look at Bill!
See Bill look at his lunch!
Bill is happy!

Miren a Bill.
Vean a Bill mirar su almuerzo.
Bill está feliz.

Bill can play.
Lee can play.
The boys and girls can play.
They all play ball.

Bill puede jugar.
Lee puede jugar.
Los muchachos y las muchachas pueden jugar.
Todos ellos juegan a la pelota.

Words in This Book

a (un/una)	girl (muchacha, chica)
all (todo)	go (ir)
are (eres/estás)	happy (feliz)
at (en)	he (él)
ball (pelota)	here (aquí)
Bill (Bill)	in (en)
boy (muchacho, chico)	is (es, está)
but (pero)	it (lo)
can (puede)	know (saber)
come (venire)	Lee (Lee)
do (hacer)	look (mirar)
does (hace)	lunch (almuerzo)
eat (comer)	not (no)
fun (diversion)	play (jugar)
funny (divertido)	read (leer)

said (dijo)

see (ver)

teacher (maestro/a)

the (la/el)

this (esto)

time (hora/tiempo)

to (a)

us (a nosotros)

was (era/estuvo)

we (nosotros)

what (que)

where (donde)

will

Note: There are 43 words in this book. RL:0.5
Nota: Hay 43 palabras en este libro. RL:0.5

What Do You Think?

1. Why do you think Bill did not want anyone to see his lunch?

2. If you were Bill, what would you have done when you found your new lunch?

3. Why do you think Lee gave Bill his lunch?

4. How many items did Lee exchange for the potato in Bill's first lunch?

5. How would Bill have felt if Lee had not exchanged the items?

Additional Activities

1. Make a card for a friend with a Bible verse on it.

2. Count the number of friends in your neighborhood.

3. Choose words from the word list and use them correctly in sentences.

4. Sprout a potato: First, cut the potato into pieces, making sure there is an eye in each piece. Then put it in some water to sprout.

5. Go outside and think about the ways God tells you that He loves you.

6. Sing a sharing song.

7. Make something to eat and give it to a friend.